Other titles in the bunch:

Baby Bear Comes Home
Big Dog and Little Dog Visit the Moon
Delilah Digs for Treasure   Dilly and the Goody-Goody
Horse in the House   I Don't Want to Say Yes!
Juggling with Jeremy   Keeping Secrets
Mabel and Max   Magnificent Mummies
Midnight at Memphis   Mouse Flute
The Nut Map   Owl in the House
Riff-Raff Rabbit   Rosie and the Robbers
Runaway Fred   Tom's Hats

First published in Great Britain 1998 by Mammoth
an imprint of Reed International Books Limited
Michelin House, 81 Fulham Rd, London SW3 6RB.
Published in hardback by Heinemann Educational Publishers,
a division of Reed Educational and Professional Publishing Limited
by arrangement with Reed International Books Limited.
Text copyright © Alison Ritchie 1998
Illustrations copyright © Paul Cherrill 1998
The Author and Illustrator have asserted their moral rights
Paperback ISBN 0 7497 3130 3
Hardback ISBN 0 434 80035 X
10 9 8 7 6 5 4 3 2 1
A CIP catalogue record for this title is available from the British Library
Printed and bound in Italy by Olivotto

Riff-Raff Rabbit

by ALISON RITCHIE
and illustrated by PAUL CHERRILL

BLue Bananas

For T.G.

A.R.

For Mum, Dad and Chris

P.C.

Riff-Raff Rabbit played the drums.

He had his own band.

There was Syd

the snake on

saxophone

and Hot Dog on trombone.

Fat Cat played

double bass

and Fingers

Racoon played

the spoons.

Their biggest fan was Riff-Raff's little brother, Ronald. He thought they were the greatest.

Mr and Mrs Riff-Raff did not think the Raging Riff-Raffs were the greatest.
Mr and Mrs Riff-Raff thought they were one big horrible noise.

When the
Raging
Riff-Raffs
practised
in Riff-Raff's
bedroom,
Mr Riff-Raff
banged
on the wall
with a rolled-up
newspaper.

stop
that
noise!

Let
me in!

When they practised in the

bathroom, Mrs Riff-Raff

banged on the door

with her hair-

brush.

13

When they practised in the back garden,

the neighbours threw water over the fence.

But that didn't stop the Raging Riff-Raffs.
They just kept on playing.

They played

in the kitchen,

the sitting room

and the hall.

They played

in the shed

and the

greenhouse.

Mr and Mrs Riff-Raff couldn't stand it any longer. Mr Riff-Raff was tearing his hair out.

Mrs Riff-Raff was

a nervous wreck.

I can't take any more!

They took Riff-Raff's drums away. They banned the members of the Raging Riff-Raffs. 'Go home and don't come back!' they said.

Out went Syd on saxophone and Hot Dog on trombone.

Out went Fat Cat on double bass

and Fingers Racoon on spoons.

Riff-Raff didn't know what to do.

He mooched.

He moped.

He wouldn't eat.

He couldn't sleep.

But the next day, Riff-Raff played . . .

the dustbins, the saucepans and the car

bonnet.

BOOM!
BOOM!

He played the television,

the goldfish bowl . . .

Mr and Mrs Riff-Raff couldn't stand it any longer. 'OK, Riff-Raff, you win! We give in! We'll find somewhere else for the Raging Riff-Raffs to play.'

29

All through the night, Mr and Mrs Riff-Raff dug a sound-proof burrow, deep underground. It was a special place where Riff-Raff could be as noisy as he liked, and no one would hear a thing.

Time for a break, dear!

32

'OK, Riff-Raff,' said Mrs Riff-Raff
the next morning, 'this is YOUR place.'
'And it's the ONLY place where you
can play!' added Mr Riff-Raff.

Riff-Raff hung up

a sign outside.

He phoned the

members of the band.

That afternoon . . .

Back came Syd on saxophone

and Hot Dog on trombone.

Back came Fat Cat on double bass
and Fingers Racoon on spoons.

The Raging Riff-Raffs were together
again!

They could play and play and play!

Morning,

noon

and night,

the ground shook,
rattled,
and rolled.

But Mr and Mrs Riff-Raff could not hear
a sound.

They were very happy.

Ronald was *not* happy.

He mooched.

He moped.

He wouldn't eat.

He couldn't sleep.

But the next day . . .